Today I am . . .
A Clown

by Jane Bottomley

IDEALS CHILDREN'S BOOKS

Nashville, Tennessee

A circus has come to our town.

So today I am . . .

a clown!
I have bright green hair

that stands up in the air
and long, stripy socks that fall down.

With big, yellow buttons and bows
and a large, shiny, red nose,

I can do lots of cartwheels
and turn head over heels

until I trip over my toes.

At last it's time to go out.
"Look, there's the big top!" I shout.

I soon find my seat,
and we have hot dogs to eat.

It's hard to stop jumping about.

Daredevil riders balance with ease.
Acrobats swing gaily on the trapeze.

Enormous elephants each stand on one leg,
and noisy sea lions sit up and beg.

Then in rush the clowns right on cue –
spangled, spotted, and striped red and blue.

We laugh at them all
as they stumble and fall.

How I wish that I could play too!

Then suddenly everyone claps with a cheer
as one of them merrily tickles my ear.

As they bow to the crowd, I am waving with glee.
I'm not sad the show's over, for, you see,

I'm so happy inside that I'm glowing with pride.

The clowns had made faces at ME!